W9-BEY-742

POMEGRANATE

POEMS BY ANITA PETRUCCI

HENRY HARRISON *Publisher* NEW YORK

Copyright 1931 *by*
Henry Harrison

To Someone
Who Understands

Contents

Boast of Time

I WAS never born,
I will never die;
Yet, while a lightning angrily
Tears across a wrathful sky,
I am born infinitely,
And infinitely I die.

Life

Out of a dream
　　A bud of time
Blooms into charm,
　　Beauty, fragrance,
　　Mystery;
Its gardener unseen,
　　A rose
Guarded by thorns,
Petals crimsoned with love;
It grows
Watered by rain,
Teardrops of rain,
　　Fed by the rays
Of a sun high above.
　　It gives
Its passion, pleasure and pain,
Then fades, bends, droops,
　　Returns . . . .
With a prayer
　　Silent,
　　Serene,
　　Into a dream.

The Calling

OUT of a limpid nothingness
  Arose a far-off call,
Into that limpid nothingness
  I heard it slowly fall.

I heard its sweetness gently die
  And melt away in silence,
As a praying breath of incense
  Melts while spiring to the sky.

I listened still, but all in vain,
  I could not catch another strain!
I only heard its echo roll
  Over the longing ocean of my soul.

Freedom

FREEDOM they say, lives everywhere,
    In silver clouds and crystal air;
Freedom, they say, is wont to dwell
    In lofty mountains, sea, and dell.
And yet, when I began to roam
    In search of her most frequent home,
I found her curled within the cell
    Of a small, pink, periwinkle shell.

A Prayer

O Princess Truth,
    Sitting on your ancient throne,
Give me now your favorite
    White ball of silken thread;
For I am venturing all alone
    In life's dark labyrinth—
Twilight shades it and I dread
    Its unlocked secret doors,
And all its winding corridors.
    But if you lend your ball of thread
To untwine along my way,
    O, then I shall never dread
That I might go astray.

Lament

TIME, you're a fine physician
    Clever, quick and kind;
But though you use your surest art
    To purge, treat and bind
The deep wound of a broken heart,
    You can't remove the lines that mar,
The ever reminiscent scar!

The Gift

LOVE gave me a pomegranate
And when I peeled its hate-proof skin,
I tasted bitter-sweets within.

To . . .

MANY lovers with gifts of ore
    Have come to knock at my soul's wide door;
But their rappings were bold,
    And their music cold,
I bid them welcome nevermore.
    At dusk, you sauntered toward my heart
Without the trinkets of gilded art;
    And when you tuned your strange guitar,
To the silver chord of a rising star,
    And I stood on my balcony
To listen to your melody,
    You played a silent serenade—
So, I threw you a rose that'll never fade.

Loveless

A HEART without love
Is a wax narcissus
In a chalcedony vase;
A neutral ornament:
Without grace,
Without scent,
Too stiff and cold
To touch and hold.

Our Love

Our love was blessed forever,
  For the night we made its vow
We sat alone together,
  Beneath a hemlock's bough.
The hemlock listened and heard
  Every tiny whispered word;
But it politely held its breath,
  And grasping us into its scented arms,
Grew taller, taller, and taller yet,
  Until it reached Heaven's star-friezed dome
And left us kneeling before God's throne.

My Kite

I MADE myself a little kite
Of tissue paper soft and white,
Then from the mountain of my heart
With childish pride I sent it flying.
But lo, it proved to be too light
For the scorning wind with great delight
Snatched and tore it all apart!
And now, my pure white tattered kite
Is slowly whirling, drifting, sailing—
In the twilight heavens of my heart.

A Million Dawns

A MILLION dawns may rise,
A million suns may set,
And a million nights may come,
But as long as Love's unsetting sun
With its utmost brilliancy,
Has risen but once within your eyes
It'll always be high noon for me.

The Flower Garden

MORNING Glories:
>   Idealists preaching silently
> To the boundless expanse of blue,
>   At noon they close their lips and eyes
> To the glamour and untrue.

Tulips:
>   Dutch housekeepers
> Who have scrubbed their floors,
>   Locked their doors,
> And all decked up with caps and aprons
>   Of the most stiffened reds and saffrons,
> Walk hurriedly to market.

Daisies:
>   Round-eyed flappers,
> Chatting, screaming,
>   Fainting—
>   Scheming.

Hollyhocks:
>   Aristrocratic English dames
> Dressed to go to tea,
>   Coming down the stairs
> With the greatest dignity.

Bleeding Hearts:
>   Maidens sorrowing
> Beneath a fleeting smile,
>   With eyes tear-worn
> And hearts love-torn.

Calla Lillies:
Brides kneeling at an altar
They have received Communion:
So they wait serenely
For benediction.

Irises:
A host of slender dancers—
Graceful toe-dancers,
Draped in iridescent veils,
A different pose—a different hue
Orchid, white or faded blue.

Poppies:
Mothers whose souls
Echo with the moans of war.
They loved all,
Had all,
But gave all unselfishly,
And now—bereft of their dearest gems,
They raise blood-stained chalices,
Hoping all.

Pansies:
An eager group of psychologists,
Philosophers and scientists
Thinking, weighing
Scanning.

Asters:
Contented grandmothers,
Clad in purple serge,

Their prayers are said,
Their duties done;
So, they sit crocheting in the sun.

Lilacs:
A choir of girl sopranos
With sweet, lyric voices,
Singing a dirge to winter,
And a short prelude to summer.

Roses:
Sweethearts
Robed in crimson loveliness,
They bend their scented heads,
To whispered words of tenderness.

Forget-me-nots:
Blue-eyed poets,
Sitting beneath a weeping willow,
By the bank of some little stream,
They are trying to put together
Bits of a broken dream.

Marigolds:
Old gypsy misers,
Twisting with rhapsody,
For they're tying in their kerchiefs
Stolen jewelry.

Buried Ivory

LAST night we spilt our crimson dyes
    And buried all our ivory,
Then beneath the desert skies
    We slept and dreamt fancifully,
Yet while we dreamt, the stars above
    Tinged 'our dreams with hope and love.

But now the far-off call of dawn
    Awakes us with an urgent ban;
It bids us rise and journey on
    With the slowly passing caravan,
Until we've crossed the flaming sands,
    And sold our dreams to desert lands.

O, shall we pause along the way
    To barter with Arabian kings,
Who'll offer silks and bright brocade
    And gilded rings that fade away?
Ah no, our dreams are star-gilt things
    No, they can never, never fade.

We'll reach the oasis of Truth
    And there, beneath the cool palm trees
A humble maiden, sweet with youth,
    Will calmly buy our treasured dreams,
Yet, not with gold and stones of jade
    But with love and peace that cannot fade.

Symphony

WHEN every soul has tuned its lyre
    To the last chord of Love,
When every world and topaz star
    Has rung its echo far,
Then Peace, triumphing high above,
    Will mount her golden spire;
And there she'll listen endlessly
    To a mellow, silent symphony.

The Chord of Death

Last night Jerome sighed, loved and sang,
    He also thought and read,
But to-night the man lies white and still—
    Where is his dear life fled?

His old friends slowly one by one
    Beside him kneel to pray;
Not even the town philosopher
    Can keep the tears away.

His little son now grasps his hand
    And sadly begins to cry,
"Wake up, O father, sing to me,
    O, why don't you reply?"

But Death has sounded long the chord,
    And Jerome has tranquilly
Begun to sing the eternal song
    In an Unheard Symphony.

My Chain

GIVE me the silver that the moon
　　Sheds on your breast, O sea,
And all the gold the dying sun
　　Bequeaths you peacefully.

Then, give me the twinkling diamonds
　　That fall in your heart at night,
And all the opals that the dawn
　　Spills from her chest of light.

And with them all I'll make myself
　　Such a long and precious chain
As never was worn, nor even touched
　　By the mightiest sovereign.

The Hypocrite

CRIMSON roses rambled round
  The garden of your heart,
So, I thought, within I'd find
  Flowers of the rarest kind
Of sweetest breath and deepest hue;
  But when I'd swung the gates apart,
To gaze within, I soon found
  That only thorns and thistles grew.

Twilight

OVER Day's curling auburn hair
There falls a grey-black Spanish shawl
Brocaded with twinkling amber stars
And fastened with the silver brooch
Of a slowly crescent moon.

To the Sea

MYSTERIOUS sea,
Now you are sleeping,
Serenely dreaming
On a bed of blue tranquillity,
On depths of priceless treasures
Guarded by mermaids.
But now, what's breaking
Those limpid dreams?
Why do you rise and sigh;
Alas, even shriek and cry?
What demon is tempting
Your fickle soul?
Bewitching sea, do tell
What makes you such a seething hell?

Windows

THE windows of our hearts are paned
  With crystal richly stained
In silver, turquoise, cerise and blue;
  For when Love sends his sunbeams through,
O, what rainbows fall and glow
  On the dark-brown floor below.

Victory

WHEN the ghost of War at last has furled
  Her blood-smeared banner,
And has withdrawn her conquered armies
  Of hatred, fear and hunger,
She shall bid farewell forever
  To the haunted fields of the world;
And the Soul of Peace shall wander
  From vale to mountain peak,
Waving a pure white pennant
  That shall never know defeat.

Inquiry

(*After seeing the drama "Journey's End"*)

"CAN it be my journey's ended?"
The dying soldier sighed.
"Can it be I've fought and lost
On life's rough mountain's side?

"The distant rumbling's fainter,
The haunting groans are dead;
Captain, is the battle over?
Are all those war fiends fled?

"But what means this thickening darkness?
O, what does it hide from me—
Chaos, chasm, nothingness
Or home and tranquillity?"

Ode

(A translation from Horace)

WHEN black clouds veil the guiding stars
And a storm is raging savagely,
The mariner lost out on the deep
Implores for mind-tranquillity.

The Medes and fiery tribe of Thrace
When frenzied with the thirst for war
Pray the gods to give them grace
Of peace and heart-serenity.

But that rare peace, that inward joy,
O Grosphus, you can never buy
With gleaming gems or luring gold
Or with the purest crimson dye.

And lictors cannot end the wars
That bar the highways of the heart;
Nor can the wings of care be shorn
With swords of gold or hands of art.

The poor man's blest who lives content
For whom a salt-plate spotless gleams,
Whom neither fear nor selfish greed
Go haunt him in his pleasing dreams.

Why should we aim at many things
In this fleet breath of endless time?
Why should we leave our native sky
And restless seek an unknown clime?

For fear climbs even brazen prows
And weird and morbid flitting care
Pursues the swiftest cavalry;
It dares to follow anywhere.

So, dry all bitter tears and smile,
Enjoy the sunbeams of to-day,
And scorn to seek what lies beyond;
No soul is blest in everyway:

Achilles though both young and famed
Was snatched by cold Death suddenly;
While Tithonus was doomed to waste
In youthless immortality.

Thus you are draped with crimson robes
And greeted by a palfrey's neigh;
While Fate gave you vast pasture lands
Where flocks of lambkins slowly stray.

And while she gave me but one grove
She gave me, too, the gift of song,
And the love to scorn in simple verse
The envy of an aimless throng.

Easter Song

TEAR down the cross of ignorance,
Pull out the nails of intemperance.

Remove the thorns of unfaithfulness,
And the piercing crown of selfishness.

Then roll away the stone of hate,
Open the tomb that bars life's gate.

Clear the darkness of fearful skies,
Then among the stars of Love arise.

''Is He Risen?''

"HE IS risen," the angel cried,
    But lo, it cannot be;
For yet on our heart's Calvary
    The Man is crucified.

His head is crowned and bent with thorns
    Of our selfish greed and pride,
Our phantom fears still deride,
    Our ignorance still scorns.

As clouds of wrath hang black above,
    We bid Him change His fate;
Then, with the bitterness of hate,
    We quench His thirst for peace and love.

We lay Him in an earthly tomb
    And guard Him through the fearful night;
We fail to seek His Truth and Light
    That shine beyond the skies' gloom.

"He is risen," this, yet, we cannot say
    Until each one attempts alone
To lift and move the selfish stone,
    And roll the weight of Death away.

To Truth

UNBREAKABLE mirror,
    Hanging on the blue wall
Of this long corridor
    That leads to some vaster hall
In the labyrinth of Eternity,
    Delay me as I quickly pass
To gaze at your stainless glass;
    Reflect me without sympathy,
So I might comb my wind-blown hair
    And might patch each little tear
Hidden in this cloak I wear.

?

LIFE, are you just a precious lyre
　　With strings all tuned to sorrow, joy, desire,
On which some great Musician plays
　　To while away his countless days;
And when those strings are broken and worn
　　Will there be silence forevermore?

"No, I am not a mortal lyre
　　But I'm the Master's melody
Which once played must never tire
　　To echo through Infinity."

Foundations

GREY-BLACK clouds will whirl above
    The temple of my heart,
The earth will shake, the wind will roar,
    And the cutting rain and hail
Will beat against its unlocked door.
    But no matter how sadly the wind may wail,
No matter how fiercely the gale may blow,
    My temple 'll remain unharmed, erect;
For Love has been its architect!

The Atheist

HE NAMED himself an atheist
    Because he could not see,
Why a Love would ever create
    Such a world of misery.

"Why should a great Intelligence
    Allow war, hate and pain?
Ah, surely if there were a God,
    His thoughts were quite in vain."

So, he scorns his brothers heart-felt prayer,
    His belief and helping deed,
While he himself summons faith
    To speak his biting creed.

Man, he's sure, is just a mass
    Of atoms in endless strife,
Without a purpose, without a plan,
    Yet, he clings close to life.

This world, he calls, a chaos,
    An accident void of worth,
Yet, lilacs bloom around him,
    And the Heavens' reign assert.

Imagination

I MEET a woman
    Along my road
With form and features
    Charmingly bold;
Her gait is quick,
    Her poise divine,
Infinite skies
    Are in her eyes.
Topaz stars crown her hair,
    And great worlds turn within her palms,
While from her belt hang bright keys
    That open doors of mysteries.

The Quest

"I'M GOING to search for Happiness,"
  Exclaimed a restless king.
"I'm bored with all this care and stress
  And this fearful worrying."

Thoughtlessly he decked himself
  With jewels, silks and gold,
Then carrying all his pelf,
  He mounted his steed and rode.

Over city, hill and dale,
  He dashed amid the striving throng
Nor stopped to hear the orphan's wail,
  Nor heed the children's song.

Thus he journeyed one long year
  Through town and wilderness;
But alas, he did not even hear
  Of the abode of Happiness.

Tired with the fruitless search
  He stopped to think and rest
When something slowly whispered:
  "Why not give up your quest?"

Then as he pondered earnestly
  A peasant passed his way,
And O, she heaved heavily,
  For she had plowed throughout the day.

Compassion filled his royal heart,
    And he heard the voice within him say:
"Give to her the better part
    Of your gold, as she comes this way."

The grateful one went on her road
    When a beggar came wailing by:
"O sir," he sighed, "I'm poor and old,
    Give me a coin—don't let me die."

Again love filled that young man's heart,
    Yet he gave not gold but words of gold,
Such words that made the wretch depart
    With mental riches manifold.

Then as the king rose pleased and calm,
    A something touched his fearless arm,
And near him bright with loveliness
    Stood the Spirit of true Happiness.

The Bridge

A LONG narrow bridge
    Spans the rushing river Time,
A bridge of joy, a bridge of strife
    Its Builder named it Life.

It rises from deep draperies
    Of the amber haze of dawn
And curves into the thicker veils
    Of the sunset's rose and fawn.

Myriads of nomads cross it,
    Caravans of searching souls
Some pale with age, some bright with youth,
    All seeking the love, the peace, the truth.

Poverty

"WHAT is poverty?
Is she a soulful maid
Bereft of gold and jade,
And priceless finery?
Or is she labor-worn
With garments patched or torn?"

"No, she's a gaudy queen
In mansions often seen,
A lady well arrayed
In rubies and brocade,
But stripped of all the wealth
Of wisdom, love and health."

Stagnation

As LONG as men but dream war
And would thrill to hear the bugle's note,
    Calling to vain glory,
    To an honored lance,
    Or a medaled coat;
As long as nations seek romance
In drenching fields with blood,
    To gain and hold
    Some mine of coal,
    Or bed of gold;
As long as leaders covet fame
With a longer and more imperial name,
We're unfit brothers of the kine,
And more mud-hearted than the swine.

Genius

A MASTERPIECE of Heaven—
With eyes that see through darkness
And the world endazzling brightness,
With ears that hear the music
Of silence, the song of God;
With hands that rend like lightning
The storming skies of life,
With fingers that stretch through aerial bars,
And grasp the myriad far-off stars,
With a mind that breaks through man-built dams
And a heart that beats away
Dead corpuscles of hate,
Dead corpuscles of fear;
With an iron will freed and clear
Unbound to make its fate.

Judgment

WHOM shall we call the saint—
The man who roams along
A pathway cleared and straight?
Or he who lavishly
Gives from a legacy,
Merely heartless gold?
Whom shall we canonize —
The hermit who dwells barred
From his brother's songs and sighs?
Or shall we call him a saint—
Who plodding falls on a dark, rough road,
Yet dares to rise, however faint?

The Violet

I HAD picked a tiny violet,
  And admired it thoughtfully,
When I asked my friend, a scientist,
  "What is this floweret?"

He began to tear it all apart,
  To scan and analyze
Its petals and its faint perfume
  Into atoms of many a size,

"What! nothing more than a little mass
  Of molecules?" I cried.
"Merely a bouncing myriad
  Of electrons," he replied.

But as we spoke the floweret sighed:
  "Please join again my shredded heart."
We tried and tried, but all in vain—
  It was far beyond our human art.

Seekers

THE miser sought great wealth;
But his dimmed eyes could not see
The sun's rich brilliancy.

The merchant searched for happiness;
Yet, as he passed along,
He did not hear the child's gay song.

The beggar went to beg for bread;
But he could not understand
That the kindest giver was his hand.

The hermit prayed for Heaven;
Yet, he did not realize
That in the city slums lay Paradise.

Testimony

WHEN I noticed the sky's democracy
   And noticed the snowflake's symmetry,
I thought, "O God, Thou might be."
   But when I felt the passion of a heart,
And then rolled out its infinite chart,
   "God, God," I cried, "Thou art."

Utopia

WE GLIMPSED a world of happiness
   Somewhere within our crystal dream,
A realm of truthful nothingness
   Where stars are what they seem.

A world where cold gales never blow,
   Nor weeds and bramble ever grow,
The land where rainbows never melt,
   Nor opal sunsets ever set.

A spot of joy and peaceful sleep,
   Beneath whose kind and smiling sky
Wearied willows cannot weep,
   Nor faultless aspens ever sigh.

Clouds

PEARL-GREY mists
Wind blown veils
Drifting boats
With silver sails.

Smiling lilies
Nodding high
In the gardens
Of the sky.

Celestial dancers
Draped in white,
Graceful charmers
Free and light.

Whirls of incense
Spiring far
Reaching in awe
Some far-off star.

Silent ghosts
That leave the sod,
Restless souls
In search of God.

T o a F r i e n d

IF ALL the skies were jeweled
    With radiant diamonds,.
And every moonlit river
    Were to change to flowing silver;

If buds and leaves of April trees
    Would become real emeralds,
And all the water of bottomless seas
    Were to freeze to mines of sapphire;

If every dwelling, church and spire
    Were gilt with purest gold,
And all the earth at last become
    A chest of treasures manifold,

Without Friendship's crimson glow,
    That the gem of love is wont to throw
O, what a darkened world it would be,
    What a chaos of cold misery!

Memory

SOMEWHERE in the depths of me
    I hoard a magic vase,
Where every fleeting hour
    Leaves some little flower
That drops from time's
    Large drafted bower;
Now, it's a charming hawthorn,
    Then, a bleeding heart,
Now, a sweet alyssum,
    Or a gay nasturtium.

To Mother

GOD took a bit of ancient earth
And fashioned you, my mother,
And flamed it with the sacrifice
Of some early Christian martyr.

Then He grasped a little darkness
From the calm Italian night,
And tinged your hair and eyes
With its soft soothing light.

He snatched from orange blossoms,
At the foot of some Apennine,
A bit of mellow sweetness
And graced your song, mother mine.

Then, from the blessed Madonna
He borrowed patience, wisdom, art
And just one atom of Her Love
And placed them in your heart.

Soul-Serenity

As THE last quick claps of castanets
    Re-echo from the mountain crests,
And gilded day abruptly ends
    Her frantic gypsy dance,
Twilight gracefully descends—
    And with a shy and tranquil glance
In every care-worn soul she enters
    To sing her soothing hymn of vespers.

Northeast Wind

AGAIN do I hear you approach me,
    With footsteps weird and sly?
What means your savage shrieking,
    Now changing to a cry?
Why, now, do you plead so sadly,
    What alms do you seek from me?
Bold beggar, this winter evening
    Go, leave me in revery.

Thanksgiving

FOR the glow of the life-giving sun,
    And the quench of the purging rain,
For the fertile fields of grain,
    We thank Thee, God.

For the moon-drenched peace of night,
    And the deep rose hope of dawn,
For the renascence in morn,
    We thank Thee, God.

For the touch of a mother's hand,
    And the kind words of the wise,
For the kiss in a lover's eyes,
    We thank Thee, God.

For the joy that escorts sorrow,
    For content in play and art,
For love and passion of the heart,
    We thank Thee, God.

Some Morning

THIS morning at half past six
    My small alarm clock rang,
I was only sleeping,
    So, I heard, awoke,
    Rubbed my lazy eyes,
And greeted a sanguine sunrise.
    Some morning,
My small alarm clock shall ring
    Again, again, and again
    But I shall not hear;
    Not hear?
    Perhaps—
Or at least, I will not obey!
For the sky without will be cold and gray,
    And I will not be merely sleeping,
    But dreaming—
A dream, too beautiful
To break for a winter's day.

Atoms

I HOLD in my hand
 Just a tiny drop of rain,
And a minute grain
 Of soft brown sand,
Only an atom of water,
 And an atom of earthly matter—
But as I close my eyes to see
 Their essence in infinity,
With just one single thought vibration,
 They spin out a vast creation:
Whirling worlds of land and ocean,
 While I become the shrunken atom
Regulating their momentum.

Death Passes

A HUGE black cloud in the heavens,
A shrieking breath of wind,
A rending flash of lightning,
And chaotic thundering,
A fall of leaden raindrops
To quench the thirsty Earth,
Then, a sudden beam of sunshine
With a calm, a peace and silence
Across a blue and tear-drained sky!

Evolution

Out of the void
    Coils of thought,
Out of the thought
    Whirls of dark,
Out of the darkness
    Spirals of light,
Out of the light
    Spheres of splendor,
Out of the splendor
    Worlds of love.

Unsatisfied

I PLACED my rod in life's old cinders,
    In the embers of desire,
When instantly quenchless flames
    Warmed my soul with a yearning fire.
The land before me was no more
    A bare and curveless plain,
But a world of hills that gently rose
    Around a mountain's frame.

Towering through a blue-gray mist
    On this giant mountain's peak,
Shone a luring silver spire
    Which at once I dared to seek.
So, I roamed alone until I reached
    Its fertile, grassy base,
When childish curiosity
    Urged me climb the unknown place.

Ignorance grasped my doubtful hand,
    And said she'd be my guide,
While black-robed Fear slyly crept
    Around my other side;
Then, with these two companions
    I ventured blindly forth,
But instead of guiding skyward,
    They dragged me back to earth.

Disgusted with such sordid mates
    I sent them both away,
And asked Wisdom and Self-Confidence
    To come and lead my way.

They led me through a spiring path
    Through mountain flowers and trees,
And then, through caves of aged snows
    Of a hundred centuries.

At last, I reached that mountain's top,
    But when I touched the yearned-for spire,
My heart became unsatisfied;
    For it was kindled by Desire's fire;
And as I glanced upward I saw,
    Through the breaking clouds above,
Another turret rising higher
    In the infinite sky of Love.

Worship

TURQUOISE heavings of the sea,
    Blending tints of night and day,
Emerald lyrics of the trees,
    Bow;
        Something is near.

Symphony of the stars and moons,
    Silence over lakes and hills,
Twilight peace on fields and dunes,
    Kneel;
        God is here.

The Beggar

A PRINCE was clad with costly clothes,
    With black kid gloves and silken hose,
He wore a watch with a pure gold chain
    And leaned upon a polished cane;
But he kept his mind hungry and cold,
    Begging in rags for heartless gold.

Song of Beauty

I AM the universal queen
Roaming yet dwelling everywhere,
Now on the ocean, now in the air;
I am the breath of the hidden rose
And the aster that serenely grows;
I'm the cloud's slow fading whiteness
And the rainbow's growing brightness;
I'm the lake's calm crystal mirror
And the cascade's joyful glamor;
I am the bliss of bitter sorrow
And the hope of a new and brighter morrow;
I'm the love that shines in stars
And the tenderness of a mother's arms;
For I'm the queen of eternal youth,
The love, the beauty and the truth.

A Hill Range

A SEA of graceful waves
    Tree-crested, green,
Beneath a sky serene;
    Each crest, a prayer,
Each trough, a low "Amen."

Dawn

A MAIDEN rises from her bed and tip-toes
    Across a floor of dusky blue,
Before a mirror she stands to curl her golden hair,
    And robes herself with silks of honey-dew.

Now she skips into her garden
    To pick a large bouquet
Of rosebuds and forget-me-nots
    To greet the coming day.

Longing

A CANDLE's burning in my soul
    With a soft guiding light.
Its restless flame
    Spiring ever upward,
Flickers but never dies.

Autumn Foliage

A GYPSY band is passing
    Through the woodlands of the Earth,
Clapping their castanets,
    And dancing in frenzied mirth.
They wave their brilliant sashes
    In the cool pellucid air,
And to the music of tambourets
    March on to the year's gay fair.

Harvest

WHEN I have nourished all the seeds
    That dropped into my garden
When I've assisted other workers
    To furrow, plough and hoe,
I'll greet the mellow, harvest days,
    The autumn frost, the early snow;
And when Death's cold wind starts to roar
    Across the lonely barren ways,
I'll not fear it like a foe,
    I'll not bar my garden door.

Fantasy

To-night I'll build a feather boat,
　　Here on this rocky strand,
And when I've trimmed it skillfully
　　With a flowing silver band,
And have embroidered every sail,
　　And draped its prow with crimson veil,
I'll go on board it fearlessly,
　　Then, serenely I will float
On the rough waves of Reality.

Sunset

Sanguine drops are dripping
On that mountain's snowy crest;
For the heart of day is breaking,
And bleeding in the west.

CPSIA information can be obtained at www.ICGtesting.com
Printed in the USA
BVOW03s0210260713

327026BV00003B/26/A